Search for a clover, discover the world.

Printed August 2011 in the United States of America

www.searchforthehiddenclover.com

Library of Congress Cataloging-in-Publication Data

Heckathorn, Julia
Search for the Hidden Clover: Kangaroo Island/Julia Heckathorn
Summary: When two children go searching for a four leaf clover on an Australian island,
they discover fascinating animals and environments on their adventure.

ISBN: 978-0-9837010-0-2

Library of Congress Control Number: 2011910492

This book is CPSIA compliant.

Photo Credit: Pygmy Sloth photo- ©Bryson Voirin and Margaret D. Lowman, Ph.D.
of the Tree Foundation, www.treefoundation.org

CPSIA Compliance Information: Batch #0911. For further information contact RJ Communications, NY, NY, 1-800-621-2556

To my wonderful husband
Who has always believed,
What others say is impossible,
Can with faith, be achieved.

SEARCH FOR

THE HIDDEN CLOVER

KANGAROO ISLAND

WRITTEN AND ILLUSTRATED BY JULIA HECKATHORN

I went to a place
Surrounded by **ocean**,
An island so noisy
From **so much commotion**.

The **animals** there,
And the **birds** with their **voices**,
Abound in the wild,
Sounding Rejoices!

There are **Kangaroos** hopping
By **Koalas** in **trees**.
And **Penguins** out **fishing**
With the **cool sea breeze**!

An **intriguing** Australian Island, **come and see**!

Hi! I'M JULIA!

I'M JASON!

Kangaroo Island, South Australia

Join us on an **ADVENTURE** around **KANGAROO ISLAND** in search of a **4-Leaf Clover**!

"I hear there are **kangaroos** **LARGER** than YOU! They live on this island, That's who we'll **pursue!**"

"Because **help** from a local In finding our way, Would be our best bet To find clovers today!"

Kangaroos are MARSUPIALS!

Female MARSUPIALS have a POUCH that they use to carry their babies!

DO YOU SEE THE BABY PEEKING OUT OF HIS MOM'S POUCH?

⑦

On the ROCKS by the ocean
Seals gather for sun,

Resting and playing
Until the day is done.

There are 8 Fur Seals lying on the rocks.
Can you find them?

"We don't see much land,
So we can't **guide** your way.
We stay by the **ocean**,
But ask the **PENGUINS** at bay!
They spend time on land
Where **clovers** must grow!
You can get there by **boat**,
But be safe as you **row**!"

So we **rowed** all the way
To the **north-eastern shore**,
Through the warm, rough waters
That we set out to **explore**.

And as we came to the bay,
Just **around the bend...**

We were **greeted by a penguin**
At the **water's end.**

(14)

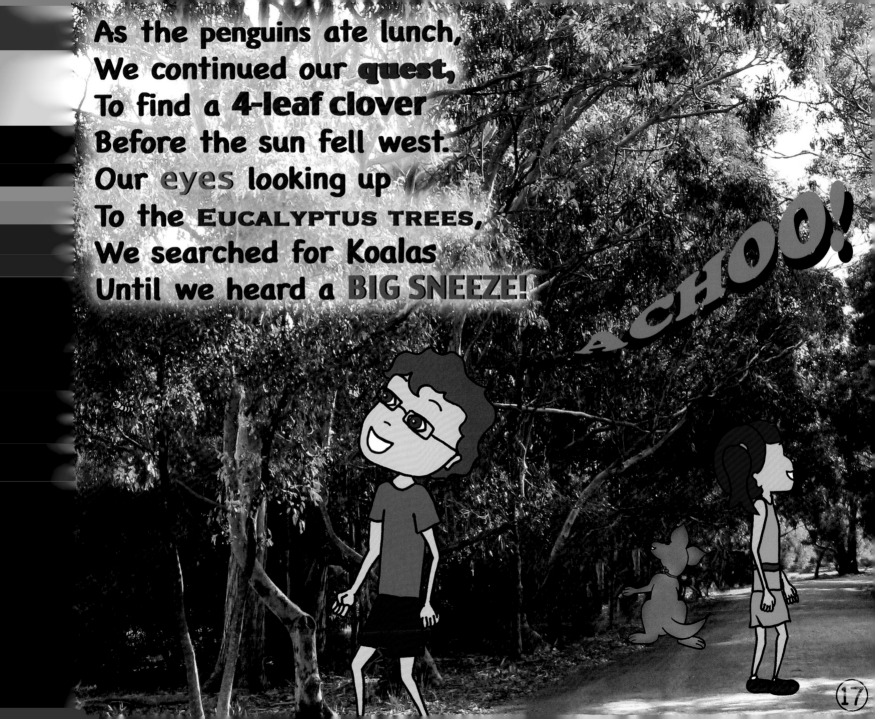

As the penguins ate lunch,
We continued our **quest**,
To find a **4-leaf clover**
Before the sun fell west.
Our eyes looking up
To the EUCALYPTUS TREES,
We searched for Koalas
Until we heard a BIG SNEEZE!

ACHOO!

"WHAT"?!" We exclaimed!
"We don't understand.
On Boomeroo's floor?!
She lives on Grassland!"

"Exactly!" Said Slow Moe,
"That's where clovers grow strong!
They'll be there I'm sure!
Now **go find them!**

...SO LONG!!"

19

Koalas eat the LEAVES of **Eucalyptus trees!**

The leaves are LONG AND THIN, and look like this

Koala Slow Moe is hungry,
but someone has raked all the leaves into a big pile!

Can you Help him find the **5 Eucalyptus leaves** in this leaf pile?

Boomeroo Led us home
As we waved **Goodbye!**
And sure enough when we got there,
We saw a **HUGE** clover supply!

And we focused our eyes
On a **LARGE CLOVER PLOT,**
In search of **4-leaf** clovers
In that very spot!

㉑

Our day was **complete**
When our **search** was over,
As we spotted our PRIZE,
A 4-leaf clover!!!

Do you see the 4-leaf clover?

22

"Would you **BELIEVE**
What I discovered today?
There are CLOVERS GALORE
Where I live, where I play!"

"They've been there ALL ALONG,
Right under my nose!
But I've never looked closely
Toward the grass by my toes."

"From now on **I'll know**
Where **clovers** grow here,
And that clovers with four leaves
Will **always** be near!"

23

"And on each new adventure,
I'll always be there
TO HELP YOU find clovers,
Both hidden and rare."

BUT WAIT! THERE'S MORE!

Did you know that there are **over 20,000 different types of bees** in the world?

The Ligurian Bee  lives only on Kangaroo Island!

There are 7 Ligurian bees flying around on pages of this book. **Did you find them?** You may have to go back and look for them!

**AND GET READY TO JOIN US
ON OUR NEXT ADVENTURE
WHEN WE TRAVEL TO A NEW PART OF THE WORLD
IN SEARCH OF ANOTHER 4-LEAF CLOVER!**

Help Save the Pygmy Sloths!

There are estimated to be **only 300** Pygmy Three-Toed Sloths **left in the world**.
They are quickly disappearing.
The Hidden Clover team is working with the Tree Foundation to help save them.

Find out how you can help by going to
www.Searchforthehiddenclover.com/pygmysloths

ABOUT HIDDEN CLOVER

Work on the *Search for the Hidden Clover* book series began in 2009
when author and illustrator, Julia Heckathorn,
was inspired by the unscathed beauty of forest on a hike to a hidden waterfall.
Julia realized that pictures alone could never sufficiently capture
the true beauty and wonder of nature for young readers.
Thus, Hidden Clover seeks to deliver a perspective changing experience
that involves immersion through books, websites, videos,
activities, experiences with nature, and other media.

Hidden Clover seeks to serve children, the community, and the world.
We have established a partnership with the Tree Foundation to help
preserve the pygmy sloth species and have pledged a portion of book revenues to this cause.
Julia and her husband also strive to regularly serve in ways such as
building wells for clean water in the jungles of Peru,
and taking care of exotic animals for the enrichment of children
who learn by the experience of meeting them.

We hope and pray that we are able to inspire others to love and care for nature in a deeper way.